For Jakob, Veronika and Maria

First published in the United States, Canada, Great Britain, Australia,
and New Zealand in 1994 by North-South Books, an imprint of Nord-Süd Verlag AG.

Copyright © 1993 by Michael Neugebauer Verlag AG, Gossau Zürich, Switzerland
First published in Switzerland under the title *Der Zwerg Nase*
English translation copyright © 1994 by North-South Books Inc., New York

Library of Congress Cataloging-in-Publication Data is available
A CIP catalogue record for this book is available from the British Library

ISBN 1-55858-261-4 (trade binding)
ISBN 1-55858-262-2 (library binding)

TB 10 9 8 7 6 5 4 3 2 1
LB 10 9 8 7 6 5 4 3 2 1

Printed in Italy

WILHELM HAUFF

DWARF NOSE

ILLUSTRATED BY LISBETH ZWERGER

TRANSLATED FROM THE GERMAN BY ANTHEA BELL

A MICHAEL NEUGEBAUER BOOK
NORTH-SOUTH BOOKS / NEW YORK / LONDON

Славному мальчику
Митеньке
в
День рождения.
с
пожеланиями быть художником
в
любом деле.

Gala Art Studio. 2009 г. февраль, 8.

Many years ago, in a large town in Germany, there lived a cobbler and his wife. The cobbler sat in his little workshop at the corner of the street all day long, mending shoes and slippers, and sometimes making new shoes, too. If anyone ordered a pair, he had to buy the leather first, for he was a poor man and kept no supply of shoe leather in his shop. His wife sold fruit and vegetables, which she grew in a little garden outside the town gate, and a great many people liked to buy her wares, for she was neat and cleanly dressed, and she knew how to display her vegetables and lay them out attractively.

These two good folk had a fine, handsome son, well built and quite tall for his age, which was twelve years. He used to sit in the vegetable market with his mother, and when housewives or cooks had bought a good deal of fruit from the cobbler's wife, he would carry their purchases home for them. He seldom came back from such an errand without a pretty flower, or a small coin, or a piece of cake, for the cooks' employers liked it when they brought the handsome boy home and always rewarded him well.

One day the cobbler's wife was sitting in the market place as usual. She had several baskets in front of her, containing cabbages, other vegetables, and all kinds of herbs and seeds, as well as a smaller basket of early pears, apples, and apricots. Young Jacob, for that was the boy's name, sat beside her crying her wares in his clear voice. "Come along, gentlemen, look at this fine cabbage, smell these delicious herbs! Early pears, ladies, early apples and apricots! Who'll buy? My mother's selling cheap." That was the boy's cry.

Then an old woman came walking across the market place. Her clothes looked rather tattered and torn, her small, pointed face was wrinkled with age, and she had red eyes and a sharp hook nose that almost touched her chin.

She leaned on a long stick as she went along, and you couldn't really say just how she did go along, for she hobbled and slipped and tottered; it was as if she had wheels on her legs, and might tumble over any moment and fall flat on her face on the paving stones.

The cobbler's wife looked hard at the old woman. She had been sitting in the market place every day for sixteen years now, and she had never seen this strange figure before. And she couldn't help feeling alarmed when the old woman hobbled over to her and stopped beside her baskets.

"Are you Hannah who sells fruits and vegetables?" asked the old woman in a harsh, croaking voice, and her head shook back and forth the whole time.

"I am," replied the cobbler's wife. "Is there anything you'd like?"

"We'll see, we'll see! Let me look at your herbs, let me look at your herbs and see if you have what I need," replied the old woman. Bending down to the baskets, she thrust a pair of ugly, dirty hands into the basket of herbs, snatched up in her long, spidery fingers the plants that had been so prettily arranged, and then lifted them to her long nose one by one and sniffed them well. It went to the heart of the cobbler's wife to see the old woman treat her choice herbs so roughly, but she dared not protest, for it was a customer's right to examine the goods on sale, and she felt a strange fear of the woman too. When the old woman had gone through the whole basketful, she muttered, "Poor stuff, poor herbs, none of the things I want. Ah, it was much better fifty years ago. Poor stuff, poor stuff!" Her remarks annoyed little Jacob. "You rude old thing!" he said crossly. "First you run your nasty dirty fingers through our pretty herbs and crush them, then you hold them up to your long nose so that nobody who saw you will want to buy them, and now you go calling our wares poor stuff, when even the Duke's cook buys everything from us!"

5

The old woman squinted at the bold boy, gave an unpleasant laugh, and said in her hoarse voice, "Oho, my boy, do you like my nose, my lovely long nose? You will have one just like it in the middle of your face, hanging down over your chin." So saying, she hobbled over to the other basket, which was full of cabbages. She picked up the finest heads of white cabbage in her hand, squeezed them until the leaves squeaked, then threw them back into the jumbled basket and repeated, "Poor stuff, poor cabbage!"

"Don't waggle your head about in that nasty way!" cried the boy in alarm. "Your neck is as thin as a cabbage stalk; it might easily snap off, and your head would fall into the basket, and then who'd want to buy our cabbage?"

"So you don't care for thin necks, eh?" murmured the old woman, smiling. "Well, you won't have one of those; you'll have a head well down between your shoulders to keep it from falling off your little body."

"Don't talk such nonsense to the child!" cried the cobbler's wife at last, vexed by the old woman's long examination and inspection and sniffing of her wares. "If you want to buy anything, hurry up. You're scaring my other customers away."

"Very well, just as you say," said the old woman, looking grim. "I'll buy these six cabbages, but as you see, I have to lean on my stick, so I can't carry them. Let your son take the goods home for me and I'll give him a reward."

The boy didn't want to go with her, and he cried, because he was afraid of the ugly old woman. But his mother urged him to go, thinking it was a shame to make the feeble old woman carry such a load alone. Half weeping, he did as she said, wrapped the cabbages in a cloth and followed the old woman away.

She did not walk very fast, and it took her almost three quarters of an hour to reach a very distant part of town, where she finally stopped outside a small, tumbledown house. Here she took a rusty old hook out of her pocket and fitted it neatly into a small hole in the door, which suddenly flew open, creaking. What a surprise little Jacob had when he stepped through it! The inside of the house was magnificently decorated, the ceiling and the walls made of marble, the furnishings of finest ebony inlaid with gold and precious stones, while the floor was glass, and so smooth that the boy slipped and fell several times. However, the old woman took a little silver pipe out of her pocket and played a shrill tune that echoed through the house. Immediately several guinea pigs came down the stairs. Jacob thought it very strange to see them walking upright on two legs, with nutshells on their paws instead of shoes, dressed like human beings and even wearing hats in the latest fashion.

"Where are my slippers, you idle creatures?" cried the old woman, hitting out at them with her stick so that they jumped up in the air, squealing. "How much longer am I to stand here waiting?" They scurried upstairs and came back with a pair of coconut shells lined with leather, which they slipped nimbly onto the old woman's feet. Now there was no more hobbling and limping. The old woman cast her stick aside and went gliding rapidly over the glass floor, pulling little Jacob along by the hand.

At last she stopped in a room full of all kinds of utensils, fitted out rather like a kitchen, although the tables were made of mahogany and the richly upholstered sofas were fit for a palace.

"Sit down, child," said the old woman in very friendly tones, making him sit in the corner of a sofa and placing a table in front of him so that he couldn't get out. "Sit down, you've had a heavy load to carry. Human heads are not so light, oh no, they're far from light."

"Why, ma'am, how strangely you talk!" cried the boy. "I'm tired, yes, but those were only heads of cabbage I carried home for you. You bought them from my mother."

"Ah, you are wrong there," laughed the old woman, taking the top off the basket and bringing out a human head, which she had grasped by the hair. The boy was terrified out of his wits; he couldn't make out what was going on, but he thought of his mother. Suppose anyone were to learn of these human heads, he thought. They'd be sure to blame her.

"Now, I must reward you for being such a good boy," murmured the old woman. "Wait patiently just a moment, and I'll give you some soup you'll remember all your life." So saying, she blew her pipe again. First, in came a great many guinea pigs in human clothes; they had aprons tied around their middles, and kitchen spoons and chopping knives tucked into their belts. Next, a number of squirrels ran in, wearing baggy Turkish trousers and walking on their hind legs, with little green velvet caps on their heads. These seemed to be the kitchen boys, for they clambered up the walls very fast and brought down bowls and pans, eggs and butter, herbs and flour, which they took over to the kitchen range. The old woman was bustling back and forth by the range in her coconut shell slippers, and the boy saw that she was really intent on cooking him something nice to eat. The fire in the range crackled and burned higher, the pan was smoking and simmering, and a delicious smell spread through the room, but the old woman went back and forth with the squirrels and guinea pigs scuttling after her, and whenever she passed the range, she dipped her long nose almost into the pan. At last the contents began to bubble and hiss, steam rose from the pan, and the froth ran down into the fire. Then she took the pan off the heat, poured some of its contents into a silver dish, and put it in front of little Jacob.

"There, child, there," said she, "just drink this soup and you'll have everything you like so much about me. And you'll be a good cook too, so you'll amount to something after all, but you'll never find the herb. Why didn't your mother have it in her basket?"

The boy didn't really understand what she was talking about, so he turned his attention to the soup, which tasted delicious. His mother had made him many

9

a good bowl of soup, but he had never had anything as nice as this before. The fragrance of choice herbs and spices rose from it, and it was sweet and sour at the same time, and very strong. As he was drinking the last drops of this delicious dish, the guinea pigs burned some Arabian incense, which sent clouds of blue smoke drifting through the room. The clouds became thicker and thicker and sank down, and the smell of incense had a stupefying effect on the boy, however often he reminded himself he must go back to his mother. But whenever he told himself to leave, he kept drifting back into slumber, and at last he really did fall asleep on the old woman's sofa.

He had strange dreams. He thought the old woman was taking off his clothes and wrapping him in a squirrel's skin instead. Now he could jump and climb like a squirrel. He went around with the other squirrels and the guinea pigs, who were all very good, nicely behaved folk, and he too was one of the old woman's servants. At first his only duties were to clean the shoes: that is to say, he had to oil the coconut shells the old woman wore instead of slippers and rub them to make them shine. As he had often done such work at home for his father, he did it well. The dream went on. After about a year he was promoted to better work: he and several other squirrels had to catch specks of bright dust from the sunbeams, and when they had enough they put them through the finest of hair sieves. For the old woman thought motes from sunbeams the best food in the world, and as she couldn't chew very well, having not a tooth left in her head, her bread was made of sunbeams. After another year, he joined the servants who collected the old woman's drinking water. You must not think she had a

water tank specially dug for that purpose, or a cask set out in the yard to catch rainwater; no, it was much trickier than that. The squirrels, Jacob among them, had to scoop the dew from roses with hazelnut shells, and that was the water the old woman drank. Since she drank a good deal of it, the water carriers had to work hard. Another year passed, and he became an indoor servant. Now his job was to clean the floors. Since these floors were made of glass, and showed every breath that touched them, it was not light work. The servants had to brush the floors, and then tie old cloth around their feet and skate around the rooms. At last, in the fourth year, he was moved to the kitchen. This was an important post, to be attained only after a long trial period. In the kitchen Jacob worked his way up from kitchen boy to head pastry cook, and acquired such uncommon skill and experience in the whole art of cookery that he often felt quite surprised at himself. He learned to make everything: the most difficult of dishes, pies with two hundred different kinds of ingredients, herb soups containing every herb that grows on earth, and he could make it all quickly and well.

So he had spent some seven years in the old woman's service, and one day, as she was taking off her coconut shell shoes and picking up her basket and stick to go out, she told him to pluck a chicken, stuff it with herbs, and have it roasted to a nice golden brown by the time she came home. He did it all according to the rules of the craft. He wrung the chicken's neck, scalded it in hot water, plucked its feathers out dexterously, then shaved its skin to make it nice and smooth and drew its entrails out. Then, as he began assembling the herbs to stuff the chicken, he caught sight of a little cupboard on the wall of the storeroom where the herbs were kept. Its door was ajar, and he had never noticed it before. Feeling curious, he went closer to see what was in it. Lo and behold, it contained a great many little baskets that gave off a strong, pleasant smell.

Opening one of these little baskets, he found herbs of a very strange shape inside. Their stems and leaves were blue-green, with small scarlet flowers laced with yellow at the top. He looked thoughtfully at this flower and smelled it, and it gave off that same strong fragrance as the soup the old woman had once made him. But the scent was so strong that he began to sneeze. He sneezed harder and harder and—in the end, still sneezing—he woke up.

There he lay on the old woman's sofa, looking around him in surprise. "To think dreams can seem so real!" he said to himself. "I could have sworn I was a funny little squirrel, keeping company with guinea pigs and other such vermin, and yet I became a great cook. How Mother will laugh when I tell her all about it! But won't she be cross with me too, for falling asleep in a strange house instead of helping her at market?" With these thoughts in his head, he rose to leave. His limbs were still very stiff from sleep, and so was his neck in particular, for he couldn't move his head back and forth properly, and he had to laugh at himself for being so drowsy that he kept knocking his nose against the furniture or walls, and if he turned quickly he hit it against a doorpost. The squirrels and guinea pigs ran around him, squeaking, as if they wanted to go with him, and when he reached the doorway, he invited them to come along, for they were dear little things. However, they whisked back into the house on their nutshell shoes, and he could only hear them crying in the distance.

The old woman had brought him to a rather remote part of town, and he could scarcely find his way out of its narrow streets. There was a great crowd of people about too. He fancied there must be a dwarf on show somewhere nearby, because he heard all the people shouting, "Just look at the ugly dwarf! Wherever did that dwarf come from? Oh, what a long nose he has! See his head stuck right down between his shoulders, and his ugly bony hands!" At any other time he might well have gone along with them, for he loved to see giants or dwarfs or people in strange foreign dress, but today he had to hurry back to his mother. He was feeling quite nervous when he reached the market place. His mother was still sitting there, and she still had a good deal of fruit in her basket, so he

couldn't have been asleep for very long. Yet even from a distance, he thought she looked very sad, for she wasn't crying her wares to the people passing by, but leaning her head on her hand, and when he came closer he thought she looked paler than usual too.

He hesitated, wondering what to do, but at last he plucked up his courage, crept up behind her, patted her arm affectionately, and said, "Mother dear, what's the matter? Are you angry with me?"

The cobbler's wife turned to look at him, and shrank back with a cry of horror. "What do you want, you ugly dwarf?" she cried. "Go away! I can't stand practical jokes of that kind!"

"But Mother, what is it?" asked Jacob in alarm. "You can't be feeling well! Why would you want to drive your son away?"

"I've told you once already, go away and mind your business!" she replied angrily. "You won't wheedle any money out of me with your deceiving ways, you ugly monster!"

"Dear me, God has turned her wits!" said the boy to himself, distressed. "How am I to get her home?" Then he said out loud, "Dearest Mother, do be sensible! Look at me properly. I'm your son. I'm Jacob."

"This is beyond a joke!" Hannah said to the woman next to her. "Look at that ugly dwarf standing there, driving all my customers away, I'll be bound, and he dares to mock my misfortune, too! Telling me he's my son! Such impertinence!" At that the women next to her rose and began to scold him as hard as they could—and as I am sure you know, market women are good scolds—telling him it was wicked to mock the misfortune of poor Hannah, whose beautiful boy had been stolen away seven years ago. They all threatened to attack him and scratch his face if he didn't go away that minute.

Poor Jacob did not know what to make of all this. After all, he had gone to market with his mother early that morning as usual and helped her lay out her fruits, or so he thought. Then he had gone to the old woman's house, drunk a bowl of soup, taken a little nap, and now he was back—yet his mother and the other women were speaking of seven years, and calling him a nasty dwarf! What had happened to him? When he saw that his mother wouldn't listen to another word he said, tears came into his eyes, and he went sadly down the road to the little workshop where his father sat mending shoes all day. "I'll see if he fails to recognize me too," he thought. "I'll stand in the doorway and speak to him."

So when he came to the cobbler's shop, he stood in the doorway and looked in. The master cobbler was working so hard that he didn't even notice him. However, when he did cast a glance at the doorway by chance, he dropped the shoes he was mending, his twine and his awl to the ground and cried in horror, "What's that, for God's sake, whatever is that?"

"Good evening, master," said the boy, walking into the shop. "How are you?"

"Poorly, young sir, poorly!" replied his father to Jacob's surprise, for his father didn't seem to know him either. "Business isn't good. I'm all alone, and getting old now, yet I can't afford a journeyman."

"But don't you have a son who might learn how to give you a hand with the work?" Jacob persisted.

"I did have a son, yes. Jacob was his name, and he'd be a fine, tall, clever fellow of twenty now, well able to lend me a hand. Ah, what a life that would be! Even at twelve years old he was handy and clever, and he already understood the trade pretty well. Yes, and he was a handsome, nicely spoken lad too; he'd have brought in so much work that I could have given up cobbling shoes and done nothing but make them brand new! But that's the way of the world."

"Where's your son now, then?" Jacob asked his father, his voice trembling.

"God knows," replied the cobbler. "Seven years ago—yes, it's all of seven years ago now—he was stolen away from us in the market place."

Seven years ago!" cried Jacob, horrified.

"Yes, young sir, seven years ago. I remember as if it were yesterday how my wife came home weeping and wailing, saying the child hadn't come back all day. She asked and looked everywhere, and never found him. I always thought something of the kind would happen, and I said so too: our Jacob was a fine child, there's no denying it. My wife was proud of him, and liked it when folk praised him, and she often sent him to fine houses with handsome presents, but watch out, I said! This is a big town, with many bad folk living in it, so just you keep an eye on our Jacob! And it turned out exactly as I said. Along comes an ugly old woman into the market place, haggles over fruit and vegetables, and ends up buying more than she can carry. My wife, kind soul, lets the boy go with her, and she hasn't seen him again to this day."

"And you say that was seven years ago?"

"Seven years ago this spring. We had him posted missing, we went from house to house asking after him; a great many folk knew our handsome lad and liked him, and helped us search—all in vain. And no one knew the woman who bought the vegetables, but an old lady, ninety years of age, said she could well have been the bad fairy Herbwise, who comes to town once every fifty years to buy all manner of things."

As Jacob's father told this tale, he hammered away at the shoes he was mending, and drew the twine well through with both hands. By now Jacob was beginning to realize what had happened to him, and he saw he hadn't been dreaming after all: he really had served the bad fairy seven years in the shape of a squirrel. Rage and fury filled his heart until it was near bursting. The old woman had stolen seven years of his youth from him, and what had he been given in return? He could polish coconut shell slippers until they shone, clean a room with a glass floor, and he had learned all the mysteries of the kitchen from the guinea pigs!

He stood there for quite a long time, thinking of his fate, and at last his father asked him, "Do you fancy any of my work, young sir? A pair of new slippers, or perhaps," he added with a smile, "a case to cover up your nose?"

"What do you mean, my nose?" asked Jacob. "Why would I need a case for it?"

"Well, everyone to his own taste!" replied the cobbler. "But I must say, if I had a

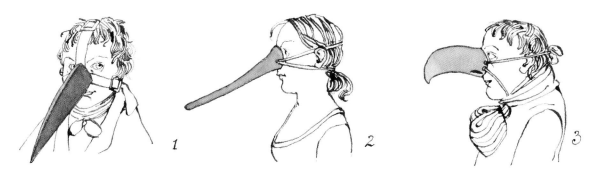

terrible nose like that, I'd cover it up with a case of pink patent leather. Look, I have a nice piece right here, although I'd need a pretty good length to make you such a case. But think how well protected you'd be, young sir! As things are, I'm sure you must bump into every doorway, and try to avoid every carriage."

Jacob stood there dumb with horror; he felt his nose—it was thick, and as long as his two hands. So the old woman had changed his shape, too!

That was why his mother didn't know him. That was why people called him an ugly dwarf! "Master," he asked the cobbler, almost weeping, "do you have a mirror here where I could see my reflection?"

"Young sir," said his father earnestly, "you aren't exactly blessed with the kinds of looks calculated to make you vain, and there's no call for you to keep looking in the mirror every hour or so. You ought to break yourself of the habit! In you of all people, it's ridiculous."

"Oh, do let me look in a mirror," cried Jacob. "It's not out of vanity, I promise you!"

"Leave me alone, will you? I don't have any mirror here. My wife has a little one, but I don't know where she's hidden it. If you're really bent on looking in a mirror, well, Urban the barber is just over the road. He has a mirror twice the size of your head. Take a look in that, and now good day to you!"

With these words, his father pushed him out of the shop quite gently, closed the door after him, and went back to his work. As for Jacob, he crossed the road feeling very downcast, and went to see Urban the barber, whom he had known well in the old days. "Good morning, Urban," he said. "I've come to ask if you would be kind enough to let me look in your mirror a moment?"

"With pleasure! There you are!" said the barber, laughing, and the customers he was about to shave laughed heartily too. "Such a handsome young fellow as you are, slender and trim, with a swanlike neck, hands like a queen's, and the prettiest little snub nose ever seen. To be sure, it makes you a little vain, but go on, take a look at yourself! Let it never be said of me I was so envious I wouldn't let you look in my mirror."

At that gales of laughter filled the barber shop again. But meanwhile Jacob had stepped up to the mirror and looked at himself. Tears came into his eyes. "No, you could hardly have recognized your Jacob like this, dear mother," he said to himself. "This wasn't the way I looked in those happy days when you were glad to show me off to people!" For his eyes were small as a pig's now, his nose was monstrous and hung down over his mouth and chin, and his neck seemed to have disappeared entirely, because his head was set low down between his shoulders, and he could move it right and left only with the greatest pain.

His body was still the same height as it had been several years ago, when he was twelve, but where other people grow taller from their twelfth to their twentieth year, he had grown broader. His back was hunched, his chest stuck out, and together they looked like a small but very well filled sack. This stout torso was set on small, spindly legs, which didn't seem up to the weight they had to carry, but the arms hanging down beside his body made up for it: they were the size of a grown man's. His hands were large and coarse, his fingers long and spidery, and if he stretched them right out, he could touch the ground without bending. Young Jacob had become a deformed dwarf.

And now he remembered that morning when the old woman came over to his mother's baskets. She had given him everything he said he didn't like about her: her long nose, her ugly fingers, everything except her long, quivering neck, which she had left out altogether.

"Well, have you seen enough of yourself, my prince?" asked the barber, coming up and looking at him with a smile. "Bless my soul, even in a dream you couldn't think of anything funnier if you tried! But I'll make you an offer, little man. I get plenty of customers in my barber shop, but recently not quite so many as I'd like. That's because my rival, the barber Schaum, has found a giant somewhere or other, and this giant brings the customers in. Well, there's nothing so special about being a giant, but a little manikin like yourself is quite another thing. Come and serve me, little man, and you'll have lodging, food and drink, clothes, everything—just for standing in my doorway in the morning and inviting folk in. You can make the shaving soap into a lather and hand the customers their towels, and we'll both do well out of it, you may be sure. I'll have more customers than that fellow Schaum with his giant, and everyone will gladly give you a tip."

Jacob was deeply hurt by the thought of being used to lure customers for the barber. But maybe, he thought, he must learn to put up with such insults. So he told the barber quietly that he had no time to do work like that, and went his way.

22

If the wicked old woman had changed his shape, she hadn't been able to touch his mind; he could sense that. He no longer thought and felt exactly as he had seven years ago; no, he seemed to have grown wiser and more sensible in that time. He did not grieve for his lost good looks or his present ugly shape, only for having been turned away like a dog from his father's door. And so he decided to try approaching his mother again.

He went up to her in the market place and asked her to listen to him quietly. He reminded her of the day when he had gone off with the old woman, and of every little incident of his childhood. Then he told her how he had served the fairy seven years as a squirrel, and how she had changed his shape because he was rude to her that day. The cobbler's wife didn't know what to think. Everything he said about his childhood was true, but when he told her he had been a squirrel, she said, "That's impossible, and there are no such things as fairies." And when she looked at him, she felt disgust at the sight of the ugly dwarf. She didn't believe this could really be her son. At last she decided to speak to her husband about it, so she picked up her baskets and told Jacob to go with her. They went to the cobbler's workshop.

"Listen," she told her husband, "this dwarf says he's our long-lost Jacob. He's told me all about it—how he was stolen from us seven years ago, and enchanted by a fairy."

"Oh, does he, though?" the cobbler interrupted her angrily. "He told you that, did he? Just you wait, you rascal! I told him all those things only an hour ago, and off he goes to fool you with it! Enchanted, were you, young fellow? You wait a moment and I'll disenchant you."

So saying, he picked up a bundle of freshly cut straps, went after the dwarf and beat his hunched back and long arms until Jacob yelled with pain and ran away weeping.

In that town—and it's the same everywhere—there aren't many kind souls ready to help an unfortunate creature who also has something ridiculous about him. So the poor dwarf had nothing to eat or drink all day long, and that evening he had to sleep on the steps of a church, hard and cold as they were. However, when the first rays of the sun woke him the next morning, he wondered seriously how he could make a living now that his mother and father had rejected him. He was too proud to act as the sign for a barber shop; he didn't want to go into service as a buffoon and put himself on show for money. What was he to do? Suddenly he remembered that when he was a squirrel he had become expert in the art of cookery; he thought he could safely say he might hope to rival many another cook, and he decided to put his art into practice.

As soon as the morning had fully broken and there were more people about in the streets, the first thing he did was to go into church and say his prayers. Then he set off.

Now the Duke who ruled that land was a famous glutton who loved good food and sought out his cooks from all over the world. The dwarf went to his palace. When he came to the outer gate, the gatekeepers on duty there asked what he wanted and laughed at him; however, he said he wanted to see the Chief Master Cook. Still laughing, they took him through the courtyards, and wherever he went, the servants stopped, looked at him, laughed heartily, and joined them, so that after a while a long procession of servants of all kinds was making its way up the palace steps. Grooms dropped their currycombs, couriers ran as fast as they could go, the maidservants forgot to beat the carpets: they were all pushing and shoving, and there was as great a crush as if the enemy were at their gates. The air was filled with cries of, "A dwarf, a dwarf! Did you see that dwarf?"

Then the Lord High Steward of the Ducal Household appeared in the doorway looking furious, with a big whip in his hand. "For heaven's sake, you wretches,

why are you making such a noise?" he cried. "Don't you know his grace is still asleep?" And so saying, he swung his whip and brought it down hard on the backs of several grooms and gatekeepers.

"Oh, sir!" they cried. "Don't you see we have a dwarf here, such a dwarf as you've never seen before?"

With some difficulty, the Lord High Steward managed not to laugh out loud when he caught sight of the little fellow, for he was afraid laughing would make him look undignified. So he drove the others away with his whip, took the dwarf indoors, and asked what he wanted. On hearing that the dwarf wanted to see the Chief Master Cook, he replied, "No, that's wrong, my lad, it's me you want to see. I'm the Lord High Steward of the Household, and you want to be the Duke's dwarf, don't you?"

"No, sir!" replied the dwarf. "I am a good cook, and I can make all kinds of rare dishes. Please take me to the Chief Master Cook. He may be able to use my skills."

"Well, everyone as he likes, little man, but you haven't stopped to think! Work in the kitchens! Why, as the Duke's dwarf you'd have no work to do, and you could eat and drink to your heart's content and wear fine clothes. However, we'll see; your skills will hardly be up to the standard of his grace's personal cooks, and you're too good to be a kitchen boy." And with these words, the Lord High Steward of the Household took his hand and led him to the Chief Master Cook's rooms.

"Gracious lord," said the dwarf to the Chief Master Cook, bowing so low that his nose touched the carpet, "do you need a good cook?"

The Chief Master Cook looked him up and down, burst out laughing and said, "What? You a cook? Do you think our ranges are low enough for you to reach one even standing on tiptoe, craning your head right out of your shoulders? Oh, my poor little fellow! Whoever sent you here to offer your services as a cook was making fun of you." Whereupon the Chief Master Cook roared with

laughter, and the Lord High Steward of the Household laughed too, and so did
all the servants in the room. However, the dwarf took no notice. "You won't
miss an egg or two, a little syrup and wine and a little flour and some spices, in
a house where there's plenty of everything," he said. "Name some delicious dish
for me to prepare, give me what I need to make it, and I'll cook it here and now,
before your very eyes. Then you'll have to admit that I really am a cook."
The dwarf said more along these lines, too, and it was a strange sight to see
his little eyes sparkle as he spoke, while his long nose flapped about and his
thin, spidery fingers waved in the air. "Very well!" said the Chief Master Cook,
taking the Lord High Steward's arm. "Very well, if only for a joke! Let's go
to the kitchen!"
They passed through several halls and down several passages, and finally they
came to the kitchen. This was a large, spacious building, splendidly equipped:
fires were kept burning constantly in twenty ranges, and a clear stream of
water which also acted as a fish tank flowed through the middle of the room.
The ingredients a cook always needs ready to hand stood on shelves of marble
and precious woods. To right and left of the main kitchen there were ten
storerooms full of everything delicious and tempting to eat that can be found in
all the lands of West or East. Kitchen folk of every kind ran around clattering

pots and pans, forks and skimmers. When the Chief Master Cook entered the kitchen, however, they all stood still, and you could hear nothing but the fire crackling and the little stream running.

"What did his grace order for breakfast today?" the Chief Master Cook asked the Head Breakfastmaker, an elderly cook.

"Sir, he was pleased to order Danish soup and red Hamburg dumplings."

"Well," said the Chief Master Cook, "did you hear what his grace wants to eat? And do you think you can prepare these difficult dishes? You won't manage to make the dumplings, that's sure, because the recipe is a secret."

"Oh, there's nothing easier," replied the dwarf, to the astonishment of one and all. As it happened, he had often made those dishes while he was a squirrel.

"Nothing easier! Give me such and such herbs for the soup, and this and that spice, the fat of a wild boar, root vegetables, and eggs. For the dumplings, however," he said, lowering his voice so that only the Chief Master Cook and the Head Breakfastmaker could hear him, "for the dumplings I will need four kinds of meat, some wine, some duck fat, ginger, and a certain herb known as Bellyheal."

"Why, by Saint Benedict! What magician taught you your trade?" cried the Head Breakfastmaker in astonishment. "He's named all the ingredients to a T, and we never thought of using the herb Bellyheal ourselves, but to be sure, that would make the dish even better! What a marvel of a cook you are!"

"I'd never have thought it," said the Chief Master Cook. "Let's put him to the test. Give him what he asks for, utensils and all, and let him make the Duke's breakfast!"

They did as he said, and made everything ready, but then it turned out that the dwarf's nose would hardly reach up to the range itself. So they put a couple of chairs together, placed a slab of marble on them, and invited the small wonder worker to begin his work of art. The cooks, the kitchen boys, the kitchen servants, and all kinds of other folk stood around in a great circle, watching in

amazement to see how quickly and confidently he worked, how neatly and delicately he prepared everything. When he had finished mixing the ingredients, he told them to put both pans over the fire and let the contents cook until he gave the word. Then he began to count—one, two, three, and so on—and when he had counted to five hundred he cried, "Stop!" The pans were taken off the range, and the dwarf invited the Chief Master Cook to taste them.

A kitchen boy handed one of the Duke's personal cooks a golden spoon. He rinsed it in the stream, and gave it to the Chief Master Cook.

The Chief Master Cook went solemnly over to the range, took some of the food, tasted it, closed his eyes, smacked his lips with pleasure, and then said, "Delicious, by the Duke's own life, delicious! Won't you take a spoonful too, Lord High Steward?"

The Lord High Steward bowed, took the spoon, and tasted the food. He was quite beside himself with delight and pleasure. "With all due respect to your skills, my dear Breakfastmaker, you're a cook of great experience, but you couldn't have made either the soup or the Hamburg dumplings quite so delicious!" Then the Breakfastmaker tasted them too, and he shook the dwarf's hand with great respect, saying, "Little man, you are a master of our art. The herb Bellyheal does indeed give everything a taste all its own!"

At this moment the Duke's chamberlain came into the kitchen to say that their lord and master wanted his breakfast. The food was put into silver dishes and sent to the Duke; meanwhile, the Chief Master Cook took the dwarf to his own room and talked to him. However, they had not been there so long as the time it takes to say a paternoster before a messenger came to summon the Chief Master Cook to the Duke. The Chief Master Cook made haste to put on his best clothes and follow the messenger.

The Duke was looking very well pleased. He had finished everything on the silver dishes, and was just wiping his chin when the Chief Master Cook came before him. "Well now, Master Cook," said he, "I've always been very satisfied with your cooks, but do tell me, who made my breakfast today? I've never eaten anything so delicious since I succeeded my father as Duke. Tell me the cook's name so that we can send   him a present of some ducats."

"Your grace, it's a strange story," replied the Chief Master Cook, and he told the Duke how a dwarf had been brought to him that morning, insisting that he wanted to be a cook, and how it had all turned out. The Duke was amazed. He sent for the dwarf, and asked who he was and where he came from. Poor Jacob could hardly say he was under a magic spell, and before that he had been a squirrel in the service of a fairy, but he stuck to the truth by saying that he had no father or mother now, and an old woman had taught him to cook.

The Duke asked no more questions, but amused himself by staring straight at the strange figure of his new cook.

"If you'll stay with me," he said, "I'll pay you fifty ducats a year, and give you a fine coat and two pairs of breeches into the bargain. In return, you must prepare my breakfast yourself every day, tell them how to make my dinner, and see to the running of my kitchen in general. I give everyone in my palace a name, so you will be called Dwarf Nose, and have the rank of Assistant Master Cook." Dwarf Nose prostrated himself before the mighty Duke, kissed his feet, and promised to serve him faithfully.

So for the time being the dwarf was provided for, and he did credit to his position. The Duke could have been described as a changed man since Dwarf Nose entered his household. In the old days he often saw fit to fling the dishes or platters set before him at the cooks' heads. Once he even threw a rather tough fried calf's foot at the forehead of the Chief Master Cook himself—so violently that the Chief Master Cook fell down and had to spend three days in bed. The Duke made up for what he did in anger with several handfuls of ducats, but all the same, none of the cooks had ever dished up his food without fear and trembling.

Now, since the dwarf's arrival, everything seemed changed as if by magic. The Duke ate five times a day instead of three, so as to enjoy his smallest servant's art to the full, yet he never showed a trace of bad temper. No, he thought everything was new and excellent, he was affable and good-tempered, and he grew fatter day by day. He often had the Chief Master Cook and Dwarf Nose summoned to his table in the middle of a meal, made one of them sit on his right and the other on his left, and placed several morsels of the choice dishes in their mouths with his own fingers, a gracious gesture they both valued at its true worth.

The dwarf was the wonder of the town. People begged the Chief Master Cook's permission to watch him at work, and some of the more distinguished personages had persuaded the Duke to let their servants take lessons from the dwarf in the ducal kitchen, which brought in quite a nice sum of money, for they paid half a ducat a day each. And to keep the rest of the cooks happy, and not make them envious of him, Dwarf Nose gave them the money the gentlemen had to pay for their cooks' lessons.

So Dwarf Nose lived at the Duke's court for almost two years. To all outward appearances he was comfortable and well respected, and only the thought of his parents troubled him. Nothing very notable happened to him until the following incident occurred. Dwarf Nose was particularly clever and lucky in

making his purchases, so whenever he had the time he would go to market himself to buy poultry and fruit. One morning he went to the goose market to look for the kind of heavy, fat geese his master the Duke liked. He had walked up and down several times, inspecting the birds. His figure did not provoke mockery and laughter here; instead, it commanded respect, for he was known as the Duke's famous cook, and every woman selling geese was happy if he turned his nose in her direction.

Then, right at the end of a row, he saw a woman sitting in a corner. She had geese for sale too, but unlike the others she was not crying her wares and trying to attract customers. He went over to her, looked at her geese and weighed them up. They were just what he wanted, so he bought three of them along with their cage, hoisted them onto his broad shoulders, and set off on his way back.

He thought it was strange that only two of these geese were cackling and honking as geese usually do, while the third sat there perfectly still, moping, and sighing and moaning like a human being. "She's not well," he said out loud to himself. "I must lose no time in killing and cooking her."

Whereupon the goose answered, loud and clear:

> *"If you try to wring my neck,*
> *Take good care, for I will peck.*
> *If you kill me with a knife,*
> *Very soon you'll lose your life."*

Dwarf Nose put the cage down in astonishment, and the goose looked at him with beautiful, intelligent eyes and sighed. "Good heavens!" cried Dwarf Nose. "You can talk, Mistress Goose? Who'd have thought it? Well, never fear! I value my life, and I wouldn't harm such a rare bird. But I'll bet you haven't always worn these feathers. I was a funny little squirrel myself once."

"You are right to suppose I wasn't born in this miserable shape," replied the goose. "Alas, they never foretold by my cradle that Mimi, daughter of the great Wetterbock, would be slaughtered in a duke's kitchen!"

"Have no fear, dear Mistress Mimi," the dwarf reassured her. "As true as I'm an honest man and Assistant Master Cook to his grace, no one will touch your neck. I'll give you a hutch in my own rooms, see that you have plenty of food, and spend my free time entertaining you. I'll tell the other people who work in the kitchen that I'm fattening up a goose for the Duke with all kinds of special herbs, and as soon as I get the chance, I'll set you free."

The goose thanked him with tears in her eyes. Carrying out his promise, the dwarf slaughtered the other two geese, but he made Mimi a hutch of her own, on the pretext of rearing her for the Duke in a special way. He didn't give her ordinary goose feed either, but fed her on pastries and sweetmeats. Whenever he had any free time he went to talk to her and cheer her up. They told each other their stories, and the dwarf learned that the goose was a daughter of the enchanter Wetterbock, who lived on the island of Gotland. The enchanter had fallen out with an old fairy who overcame him by tricks and cunning, and in revenge the old fairy turned Mimi into a goose and brought her far away to this place. When Dwarf Nose had told her his own story, she said, "I know something about these things; my father has taught me and my sisters a certain amount of magic—as much as he is allowed to pass on, that is. The story of the quarrel over the basket of herbs, your sudden transformation when you smelled that little plant, and some of the things you tell me the old woman said, make me think that the spell cast on you worked through herbs. In that case, if you find the herb the fairy used in her enchantments, then you can break the spell." This was not much comfort to the dwarf, for where was he to find that herb? Still, he thanked Mimi, and felt a glimmer of hope.

Around this time the Duke was visited by a Prince who lived nearby and was a friend of his. Summoning Dwarf Nose, the Duke told him, "Now's the time for you to show whether you are my faithful servant and a master of your art. This Prince who has come to see me is famous for enjoying finer foods than anyone else except me, and he is a wise man who knows a great deal about good cooking. So make sure that the food served at my table every day amazes him more and more. And you must not serve the same dish twice while he is here, on pain of my displeasure. You may tell my treasurer to give you whatever you need. Even if you have to fry gold and diamonds in lard, do it! I'd rather impoverish myself than have to blush before him."

So said the Duke, and the dwarf replied, bowing very correctly, "It will be as you say, my lord! God willing, I'll do all I can to please this Prince's fine palate." So now the little cook drew on all the resources of his art. He spared neither his master's treasury nor himself. He could be seen wrapped in clouds of smoke and fire all day, and his voice kept echoing through the vaults of the kitchens, for he had all the kitchen boys and under cooks at his command.

The foreign Prince had been staying with the Duke for fourteen days, living a life of pleasure and luxury. They ate no fewer than five times a day, and the Duke was well satisfied with the dwarf's art, for he saw from his guest's face that the Prince was pleased. On the fifteenth day, however, the Duke had Dwarf Nose summoned to his table, introduced him to his guest, and asked the Prince how he liked the dwarf's cooking.

"You are a wonderful cook," replied the foreign Prince, "and you know how to serve a good meal. In all the time I've been here, you haven't served the same dish twice, and everything has been very well prepared. But tell me, why have you waited so long to give us the queen of all dishes, Sovereign Pie?"

The dwarf was dismayed, for he had never heard of this queen of pies before. However, pulling himself together, he replied, "My lord, I hoped you were going to grace this court much longer with your presence, for what would the cook

serve up in celebration of your glory on the day of your departure but the queen of pies?"

"Indeed?" put in the Duke, laughing. "So, I suppose you were going to wait until the day I died before you served it to me, were you? You've never made Sovereign Pie for me, either. However, you must think of another dish to serve my guest when he leaves, because I want that pie on my table tomorrow."

"Just as you say, my lord!" replied the dwarf, and he went away.

But he was not happy, for the day of his shame and misfortune had come. He had no idea how to make Sovereign Pie. So he went to his room and wept over his sad fate. Then the goose Mimi, who was allowed to roam free in his apartment, came up to him and asked what was wrong. "Dry your tears," she said when she heard about the Sovereign Pie. "That dish was often served at my father's table, and I know more or less what you need to make it: you take this and that ingredient, and so much of this and so much of that, and if that's not quite all that should go in it, well, I'm sure the gentlemen don't have such fine palates that they'll notice."

When Mimi said that, the dwarf jumped for joy, blessing the day he had bought the goose, and he set about making the queen of pies. First he made a small trial pie, and it tasted delicious. He gave the First Head Cook a piece to taste, and yet again the Head Cook praised his art to the skies.

Next day he made a larger pie, and sent it to table hot from the oven, after decorating it with garlands of flowers. Then he put on his best clothes and went to the dining hall. When he came in the Head Carver was busy cutting up the pie and serving it to the Duke and his guest on a silver platter. The Duke took a good mouthful, raised his eyes to the ceiling, and when he had swallowed, he said, "Aha! This is rightly called the queen of pies, and my dwarf is the king of cooks, too! Don't you agree, my dear friend?"

His guest took several small mouthfuls, tasted and tried them carefully, and he smiled a mysterious, mocking smile. "This pie is very nicely made," he replied,

pushing his plate away, "but it isn't quite Sovereign Pie. I thought as much."
Displeased, the Duke frowned, and his face went red with shame. "You wretched
dwarf!" he cried. "How dare you do this to your master? Do you want me to
chop your big head off as punishment for your bad cooking?"

"Oh, my lord, for heaven's sake: I made the dish by the rules of the art of
cookery, and I'm sure there can't be anything wrong with it!" said the dwarf,
trembling.

"You lie, you rascal," replied the Duke, spurning him with his foot, "or my
guest wouldn't say there was! I'll have you chopped into bits and baked in
a pie yourself!"

"Have mercy!" cried the dwarf, sliding over to the
Prince on his knees and clutching his feet. "Tell me what the
dish still needs to please your palate! Don't let me die
for a handful of meat and flour."

"It won't help you much if I do tell you, my dear
Dwarf Nose," replied the guest, laughing. "I
suspected yesterday that you couldn't make this
dish like my own cook. You must know that the
missing ingredient is a little herb unknown in
this country, the herb Sneezewell. Without that
herb, the pie isn't properly seasoned, and your
master will never eat it as I do."

At this the Duke lost his temper. "Oh yes I will,"
he cried, his eyes flashing. "I swear on my
father's grave, either I'll show you that pie
cooked to your liking tomorrow—or I'll show
you this fellow's head on the point of a spear
above my palace gates. Off you go, you wretch.
I'll give you another twenty-four hours' grace."

When the Duke said that, the dwarf went back to his own little room weeping, told the goose of his sad fate, and said he would surely die, because he had never heard of the herb. "If that's all," she said, "then I can help you. My father taught me to know every herb in the world. At any other time of the month you might indeed have been doomed to die, but luckily there's a new moon tonight, and the herb flowers at the time of the new moon. Tell me, are there any old chestnut trees near the palace?"

"Oh yes!" replied Dwarf Nose, feeling more cheerful. "There's a whole stand of them beside the lake, two hundred paces from the palace. But why chestnut trees?"

"The herb flowers only beneath old chestnut trees," said Mimi, "so let's waste no time in going to look for what you need. Carry me outside and put me down out of doors, and I'll help you look."

He did as she said, and went to the palace gates with her. However, the gatekeeper barred their way with his gun, saying, "My poor Dwarf Nose, it's all up with you. I have strict orders not to let you out of the palace."

"But can't I go into the garden?" asked the dwarf. "Be good enough to send one of your men to the Lord High Steward, to ask if I'm not allowed out into the garden to look for herbs."

The gatekeeper did as he asked, and his request was granted, for the garden had high walls and no one could possibly escape from it. Once Dwarf Nose was out of doors with the goose, he put her down carefully, and she walked quickly ahead of him to the lake where the chestnut trees grew. He followed her, but he was heavy at heart, for this was his one last hope, and if she failed to find the herb, he had made up his mind that he would rather drown himself in the lake than be beheaded. The goose searched in vain; she wandered around under all the chestnut trees, she turned every blade of grass over with her beak, but there was nothing to be found. She began to weep out of pity and fear, for already the darkness was gathering and it was getting harder to make out anything

around them. Then the dwarf happened to cast a glance across the lake, and suddenly he cried, "Look, look, there's another big old tree on the other side of the lake. Let's go and see if my luck is flowering there." The goose hopped and fluttered ahead of him, and he ran after her as fast as his little legs would go. The chestnut tree cast a great shadow and it was so dark all around that you could hardly make out anything, but suddenly the goose stopped, flapped her wings for joy, and then plunged her head swiftly into the tall grass and picked something, which she passed daintily in her beak to the astonished Dwarf Nose. "This is the herb," she said, "and there's plenty of it growing here, so that you need never run out."

The dwarf looked thoughtfully at the herb. A sweet fragrance rising from it to his nostrils unexpectedly reminded him of the scene of his enchantment. The stems and leaves of the herb were blue-green, the flower was scarlet laced with yellow.

"Praise be to God!" he cried at last. "What a miracle! Mimi, I believe this is the very same herb that turned me from a squirrel to my present wretched shape. Shall I try it and see what happens?"

"Not yet," said the goose. "Take a handful of the herb with you. Let's go to your room to fetch your money and all your other possessions, and then we'll try the power of the herb!"

They did as she said and went back to the dwarf's room, and his heart was beating audibly with expectation. When he had made a bundle of the fifty or sixty ducats he had saved and a few clothes and shoes, he said, "God willing, let me be free of this burden." Then he plunged his nose deep into the herbs and breathed in their fragrance.

Then there was a pulling and a cracking in all his limbs; he felt his head rise above his shoulders, he squinted down at his nose and saw it growing smaller and smaller, while his back and his chest began to straighten out and his legs grew longer.

The goose watched all this in amazement. "Oh, how tall and handsome you are!" she cried. "Thanks be to God, there's none of your old self left about you!" Jacob was delighted, and he clasped his hands and prayed. But in his joy he did not forget all he owed the goose Mimi; his heart urged him to go straight to his parents, but gratitude helped him overcome that wish, and he said, "I have you and no one else to thank for my return to myself! I'd never have found this herb without you, and I'd have had to stay a dwarf for ever, or even perish at the hands of the executioner. So now I will repay you, and take you to your father. With his great knowledge of magic, he'll easily be able to break the spell on you." The goose shed tears of joy and accepted his offer.

Jacob, unrecognized, had no difficulty in getting out of the palace with the goose, and he set off in the direction of the seashore, to leave for Mimi's home. What more is there to tell? They made their journey successfully. Wetterbock broke the spell on his daughter and sent Jacob home laden with gifts. Jacob came back to his own town again, and his parents were delighted to recognize the handsome young man as their long-lost son. With the presents Wetterbock had given him to take home, Jacob bought himself a shop and became rich and happy.

I will add only one more thing: there was a great commotion after his disappearance from the Duke's palace, for the next day, when the Duke was about to keep his word and have the dwarf's head cut off if he hadn't found the herbs, he was nowhere to be found. The Prince said the Duke had let him escape in secret, so as not to lose his best cook, and accused him of breaking his word. This led to a great war between the two rulers, which has gone down in history under the name of the War of Herbs. Many a battle was fought, but they made peace in the end, and it was called the Peace of the Pie, because at the banquet to celebrate the end of the conflict the Prince's cook made Sovereign Pie, the queen of pies, and the Duke enjoyed it very much indeed. Small causes, as we see, often have great consequences, and this is the story of Dwarf Nose.

Wilhelm Hauff was born in Stuttgart, Germany, in 1802. Although he died before he was 25, his collected works fill more than 30 volumes. During his brief life he was considered a literary phenomenon—writing historical novels, satire, poetry, and monographs—but he is best remembered today for finely crafted fairy tales, influenced by his extensive knowledge of European and Arabian folklore.

The fairy tales that were popular during Hauff's lifetime were strongly rooted in the romantic period of German literature, far removed from everyday life. Hauff's tales were more grounded in reality and often dealt with the dark side of human nature.

In Dwarf Nose, *for example, Hauff depicts contemporary petit-bourgeois mentality.* Dwarf Nose *first appeared in* The Sheikh of Alexandria and His Slaves, *published in Germany in 1827. The tales in the book were connected by a framework story that set the scene, much like the structure of* The Arabian Nights—*a book from which Hauff derived much inspiration. Stringing tales together like this was a device Hauff used more than once; he had published another set called* The Inn in the Spessart Forest *the year before, in what he called his* Fairy Tale Almanac *for 1826. The* Sheikh of Alexandria and His Slaves *appeared in his* Fairy Tale Almanac *for 1827. Perhaps Hauff would have gone on to produce a collection of stories every year, but he died in November 1827, soon after the birth of his only child and just ten days before his twenty-fifth birthday. As the title suggests,* The Sheikh of Alexandria and His Slaves *has an Oriental setting for the framework story, but* Dwarf Nose *is told by an old slave who comes from "the land of the Franks," meaning Western Europe— particularly parts of what are now Germany and France. The slave begins by telling the Sheikh that "people who believe there were never any fairies and enchanters except in the days of Harun Al-Rashid, Caliph of Baghdad, are very much mistaken.... There are still fairies today, and not so very long ago I myself witnessed an incident in which the genies clearly played a part, as I will now relate." Then he tells the story of young Jacob and the spell that turns him into an ugly dwarf, and when he finishes, the whole company discusses the art of storytelling and agrees that "there is a special pleasure in listening to a story."*

LISBETH ZWERGER

Ever since she was a student in Vienna, Lisbeth Zwerger has known that she wanted to be a picture book illustrator. At that time, in the 1970s, she was often warned about the difficulties of finding work as an illustrator, and was also frequently criticized for painting in a traditional style.

"That used to confuse me," she says. "I didn't know which way to go as a painter." She almost gave up all hopes of illustrating, limiting herself to occasional pen-and-ink drawings. One day, by chance, a friend gave her a picture book illustrated by Arthur Rackham. "The light finally dawned on me. I buried my doubts, and followed my desire to illustrate books."

These days, Lisbeth Zwerger's publisher encourages her to follow her instincts. She has a strong preference for classical stories that have as much charm and historical character as Vienna, the city where she was born. In the last sixteen years, Lisbeth Zwerger has illustrated twenty books, from E.T.A. Hoffmann's The Strange Child, *to* Dwarf Nose *by Wilhelm Hauff, the book you hold in your hand. She has received many awards at home and abroad.*

In 1990, she won the most important prize for her collected works—the internationally renowned Hans Christian Andersen Lifetime Achievement Award.

The Art of Lisbeth Zwerger, *a catalog of her work to date, has been published by North-South Books and is available from your local bookstore or library. The book contains more than 100 full-color reproductions of paintings, as well as sketches, photographs, commentary, and a complete bibliography.*

THE FOLLOWING BOOKS ILLUSTRATED BY LISBETH ZWERGER ARE AVAILABLE IN ENGLISH:

AESOP   Twelve Fables (1989)

HANS CHRISTIAN ANDERSEN

Hans Christian Andersen's Fairy Tales (1991)

The Nightingale (1984)

The Swineherd (1982)

Thumbeline (1980)

CLEMENS BRENTANO   The Legend of Rosepetal (1978)

CHARLES DICKENS   A Christmas Carol (1988)

JACOB & WILHELM GRIMM

Hansel and Gretel (1979)

Little Red Riding Hood (1983)

The Seven Ravens (1981)

WILHELM HAUFF   Dwarf Nose (1993)

O. HENRY   The Gift of the Magi (1982)

E.T.A. HOFFMANN

The Nutcracker (1979)

The Strange Child (1977)

HEINZ JANISCH   The Merry Pranks of Till Eulenspiegel (1990)

E. NESBIT   The Deliverers of their Country (1985)

OSCAR WILDE

The Canterville Ghost (1986)

The Selfish Giant (1984)

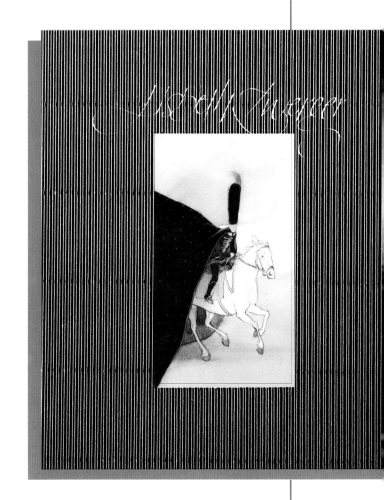